For my parents, who always encouraged me to dream.

Original comic & story developed by Travis Hanson
Adopted from the Novel The Lost Prince of Darkleaf by Travis Hanson & Aimee Duncan

Copyright © 2012 All Rights Reserved, Travis Hanson & Bean Leaf Press. Unauthorized reproduction except for the purpose of review is prohibited by law. Title logo, Bean Leaf Press Logo and all characters and art are copyright © 2002 by Travis Hanson. The chapters in this book were originally published in the comic book The Bean and are copyright © 2002 by Travis Hanson.

For contact information, subscription or letters to the artist, please send all inquiries to
Bean Leaf Press
P.O. Box 6495
Moreno Valley CA 92554

Softcover ISBN 978-1-4507-9717-7
Printed in USA
Special thanks to Becci for the book edits.

the BEAN

Broken Souls

by Travis Hanson

from the novel the Lost Prince of Darkleaf by Travis Hanson & Aimee Duncan
original story by Travis Hanson

Tears in the Dark

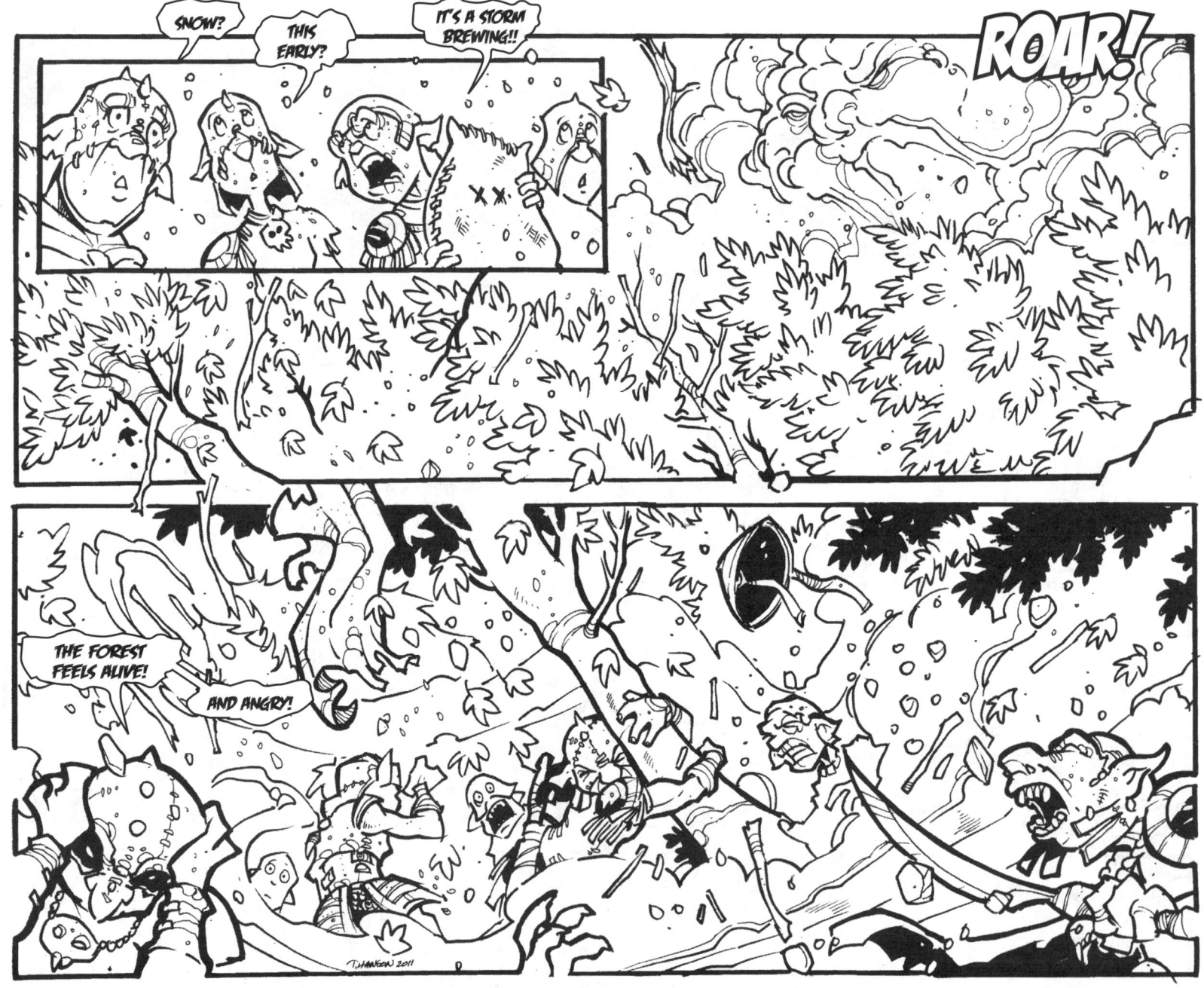

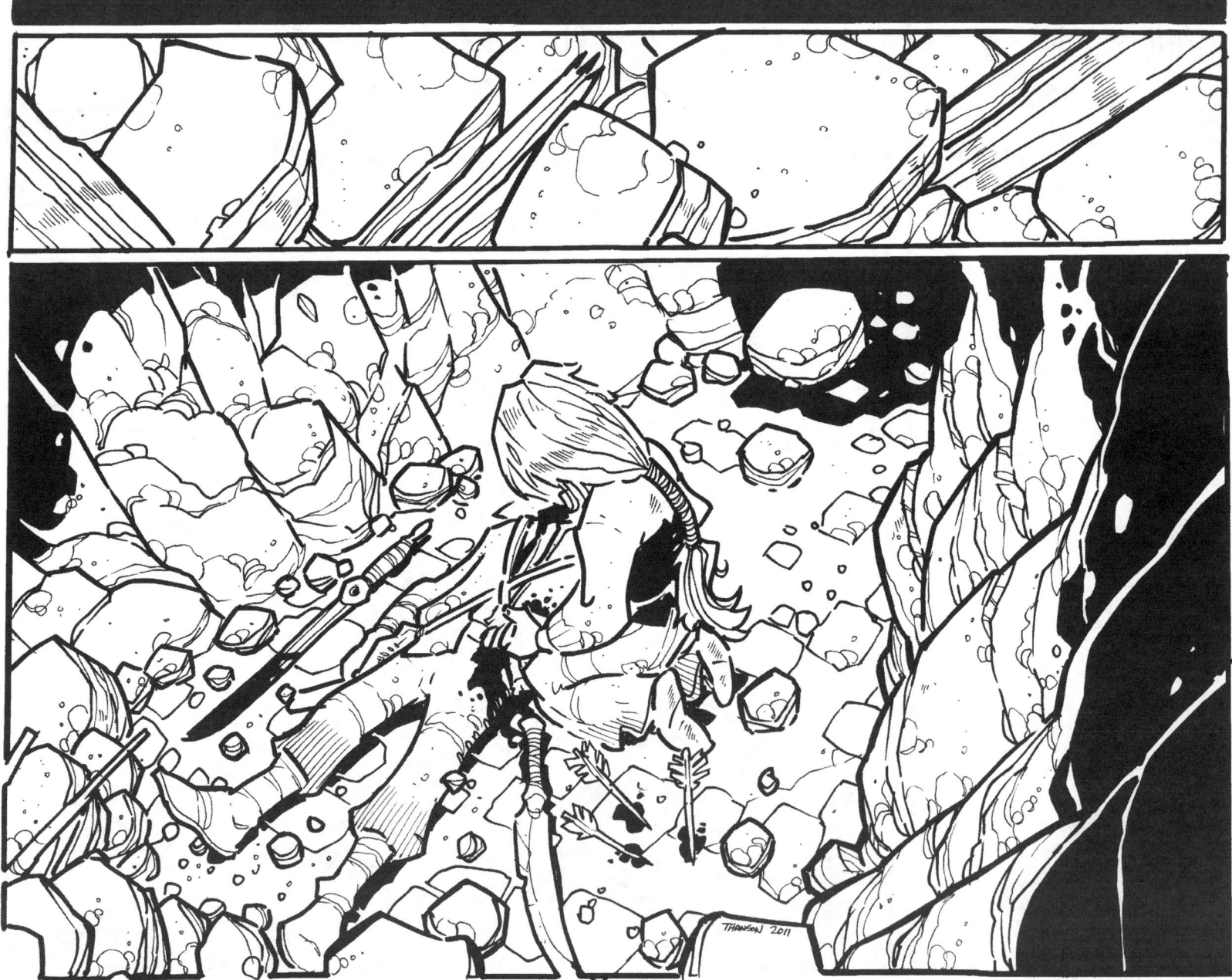

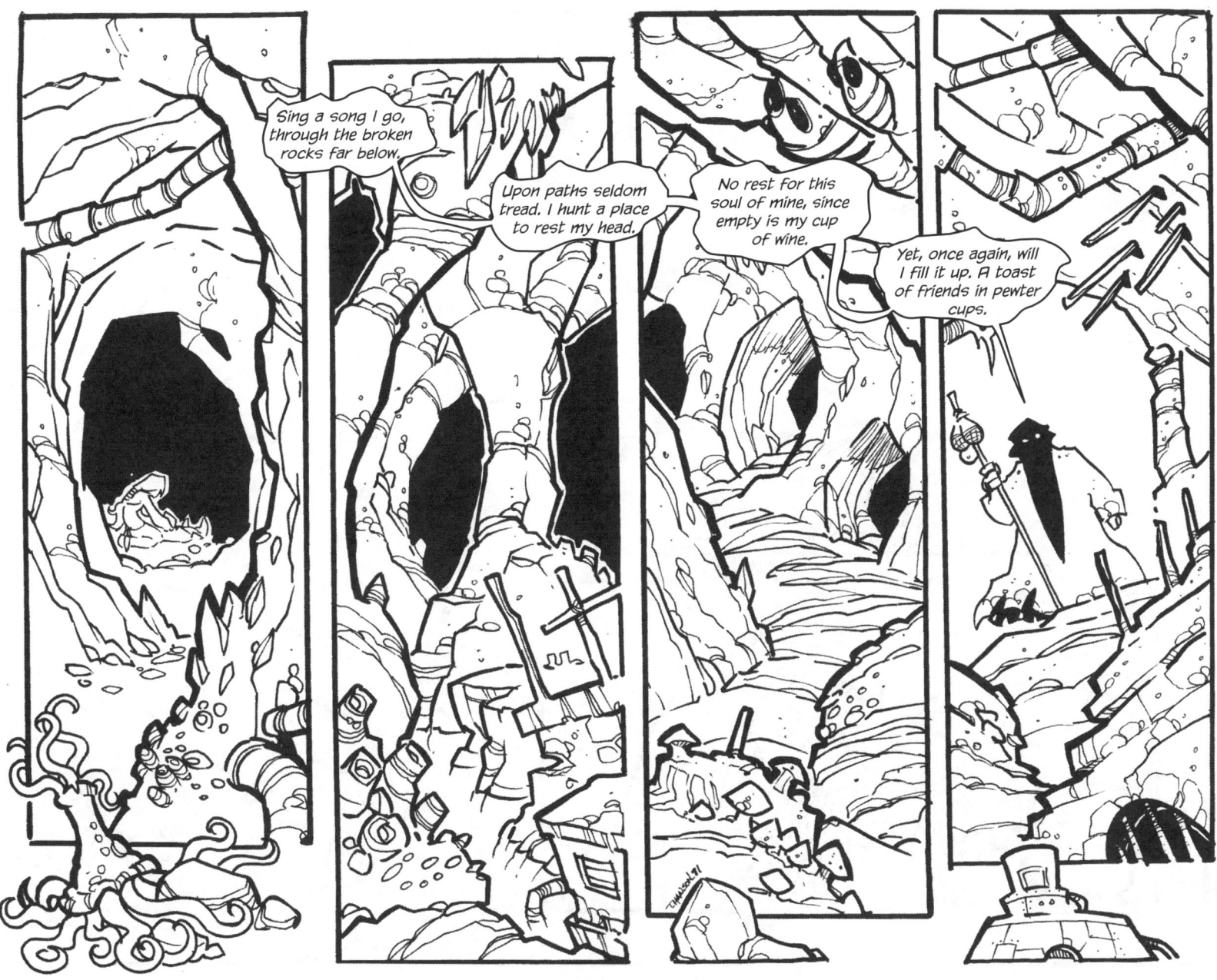

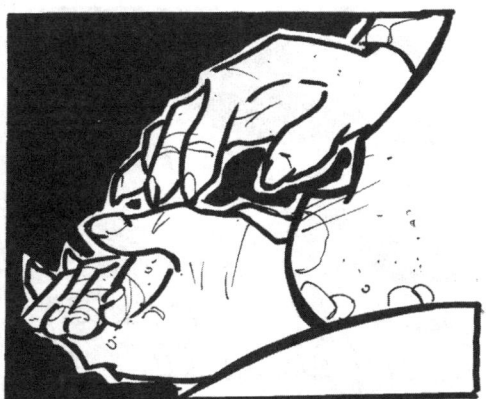

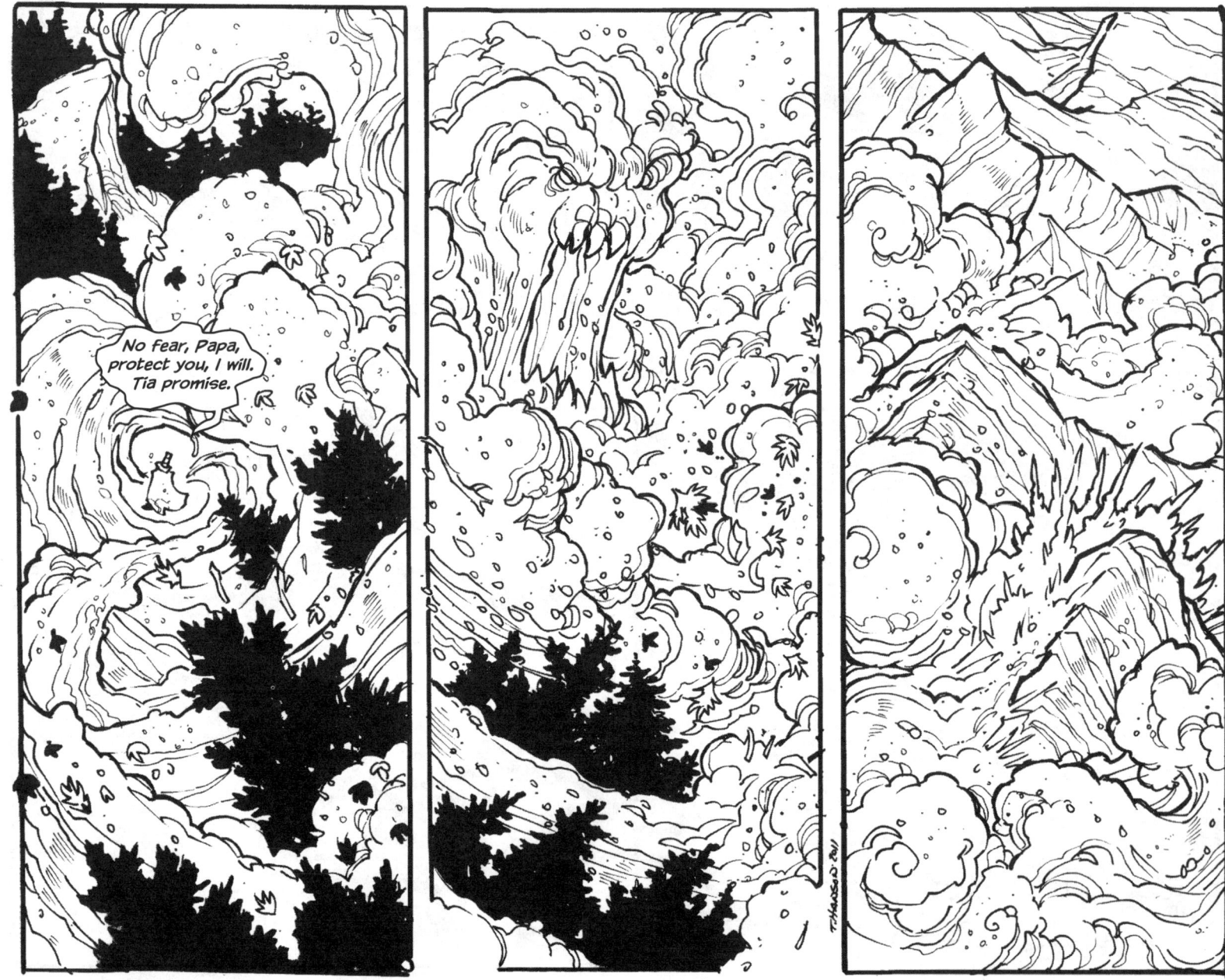

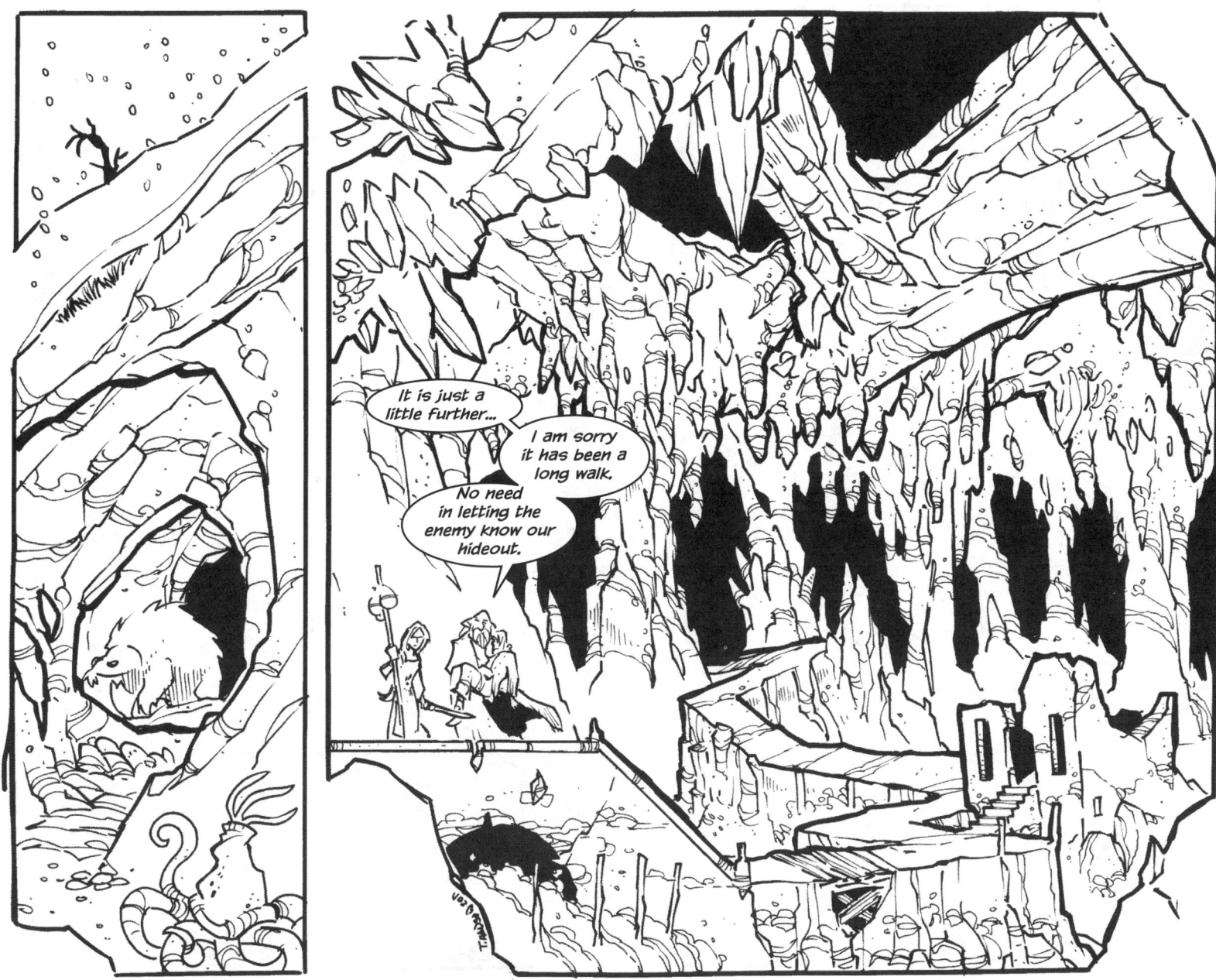

thaddeus

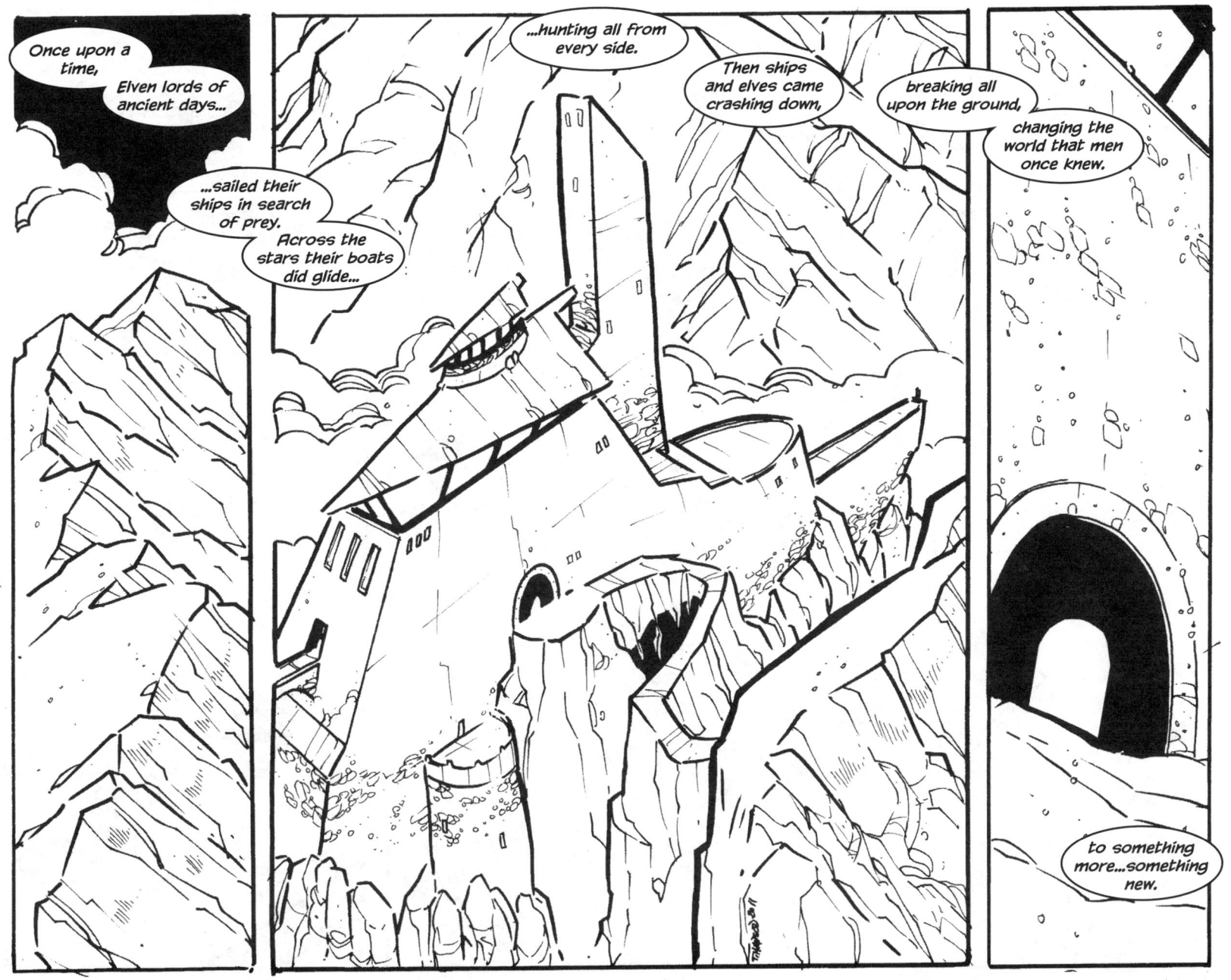

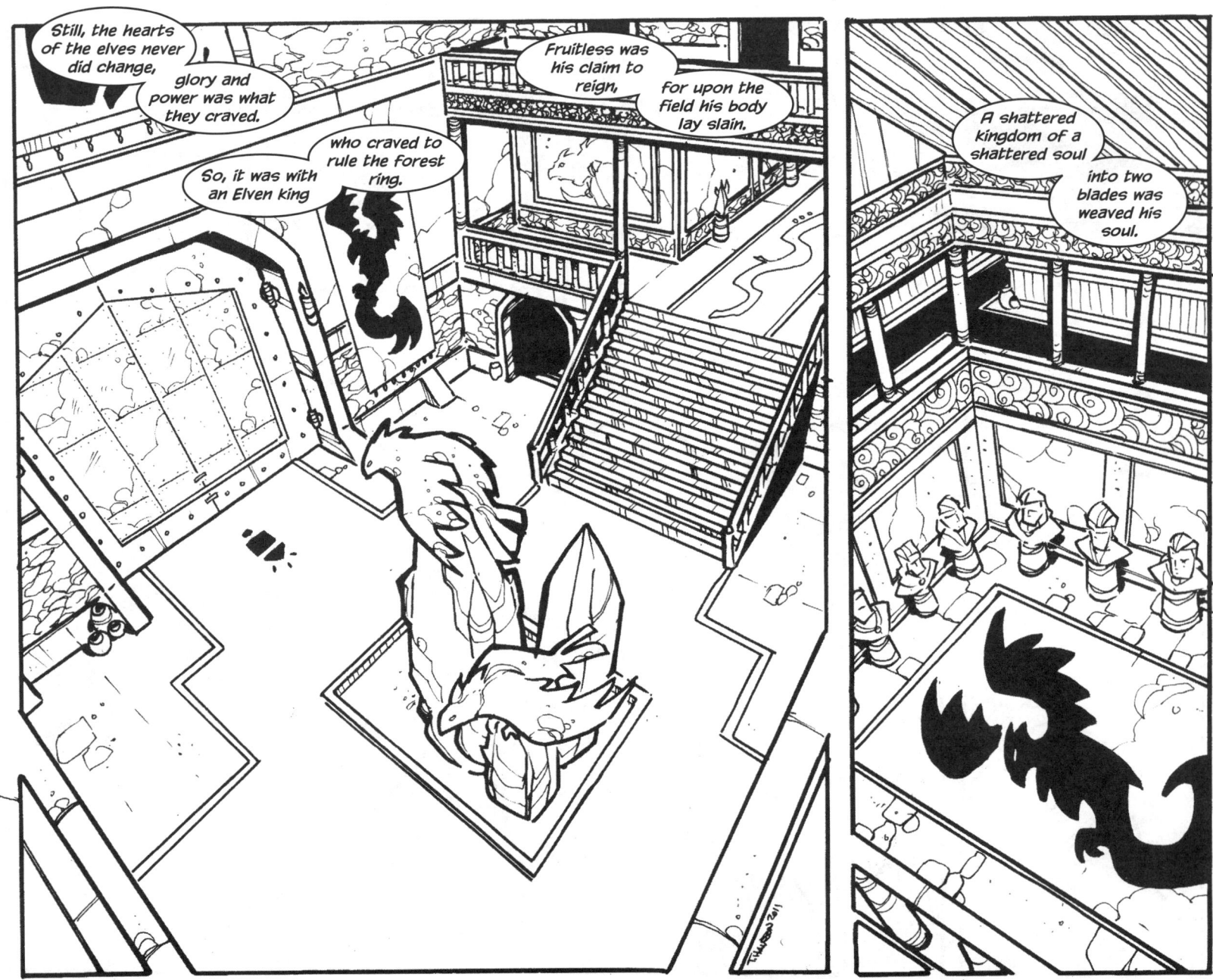

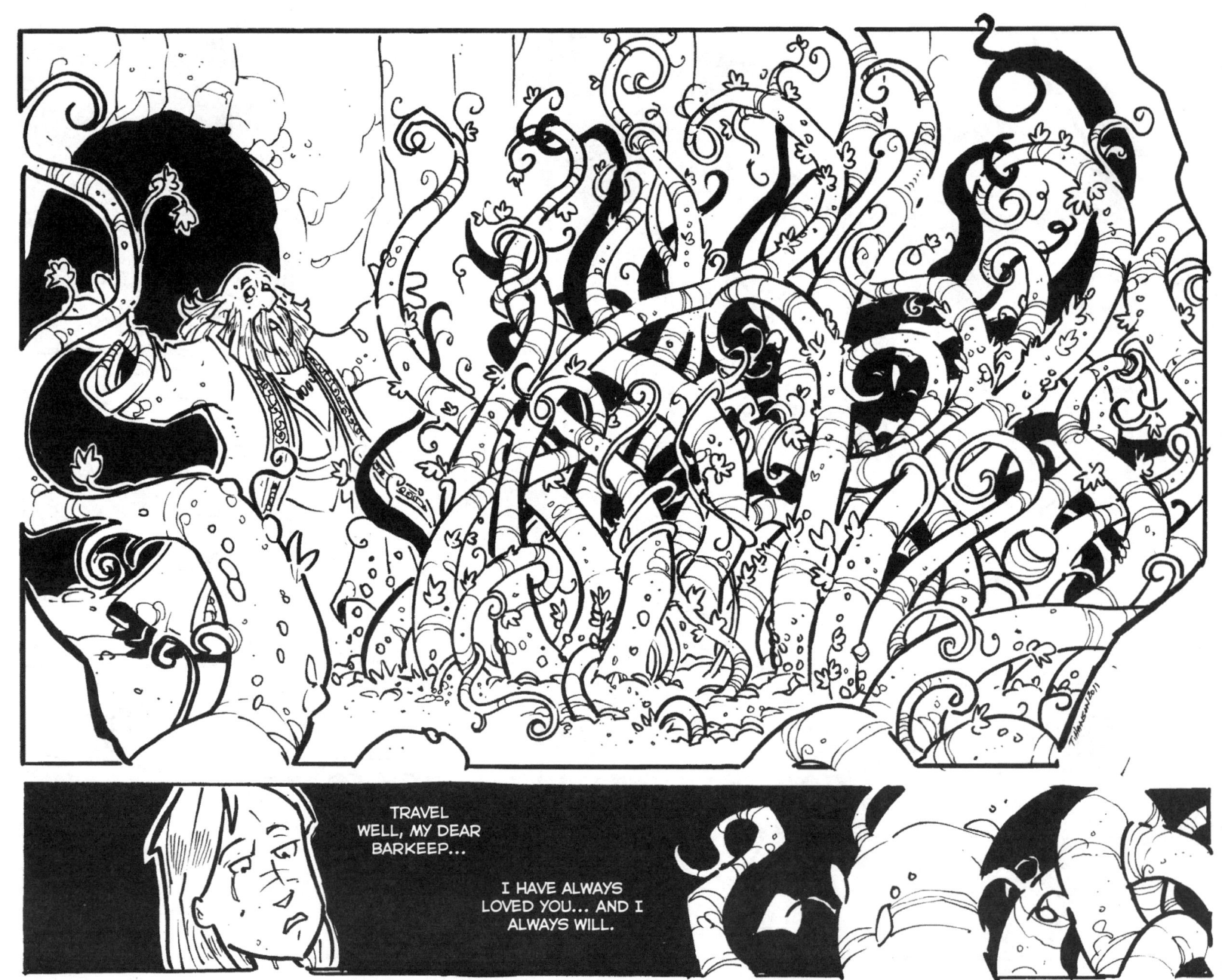

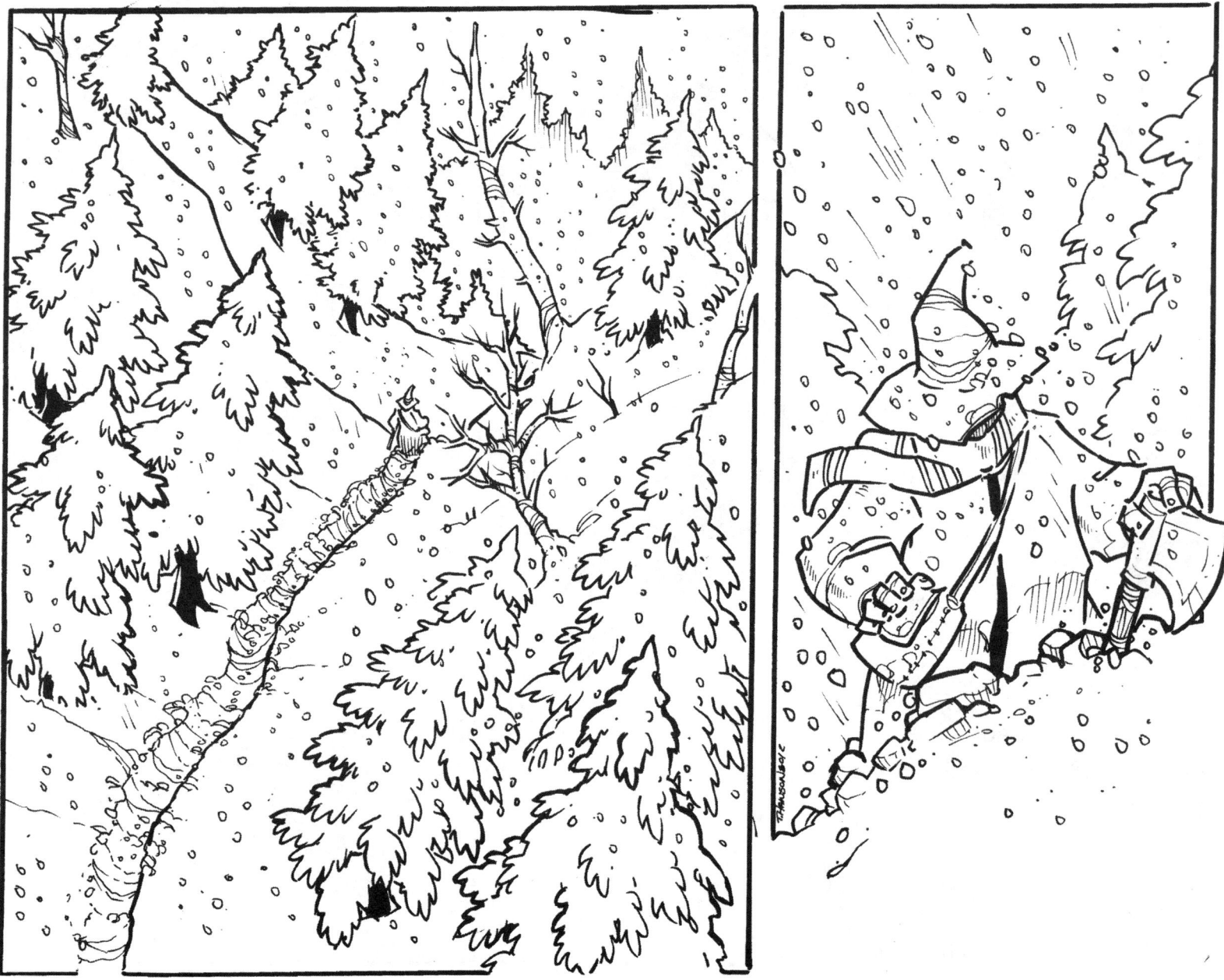

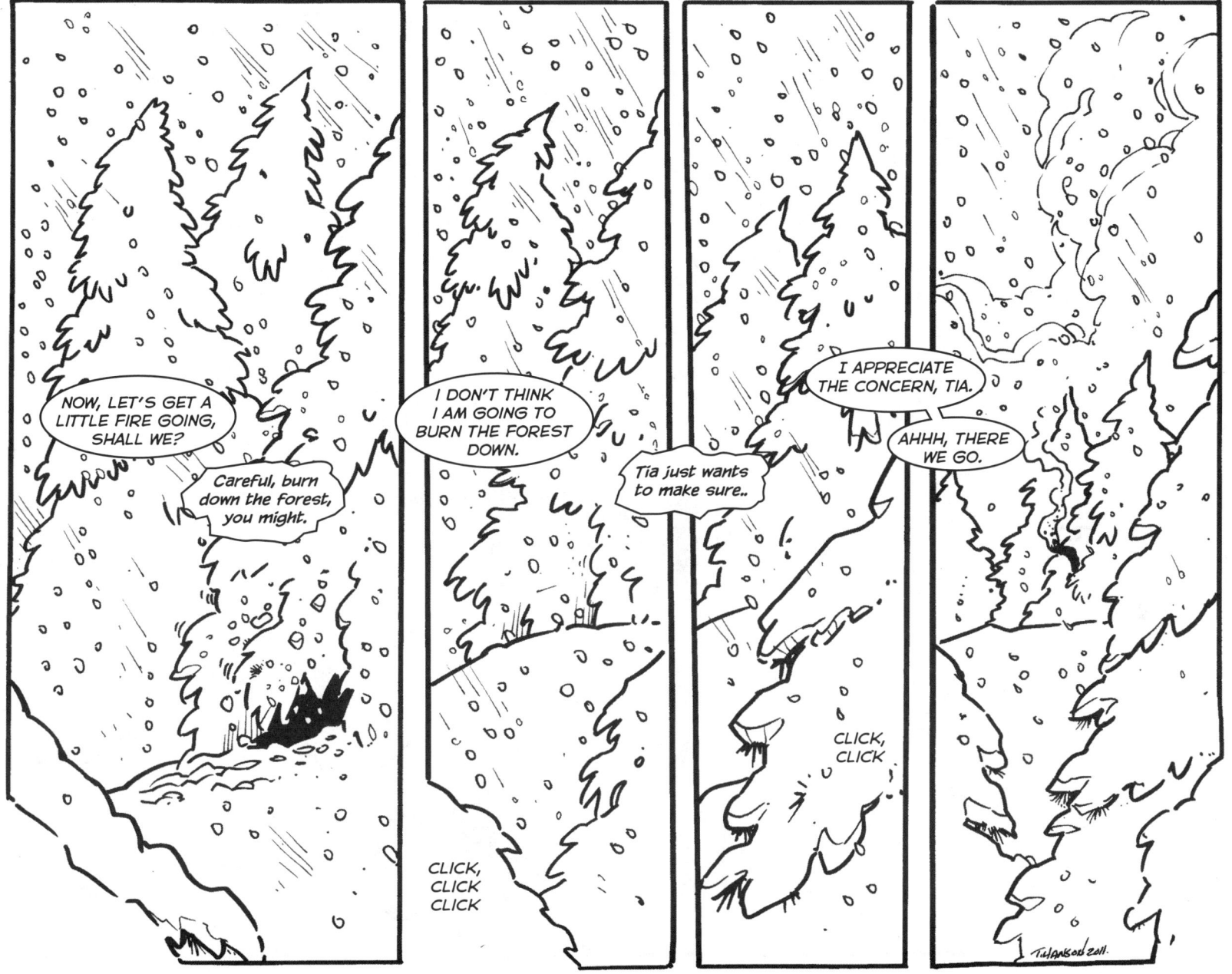

the Watcher of the Broken Moon

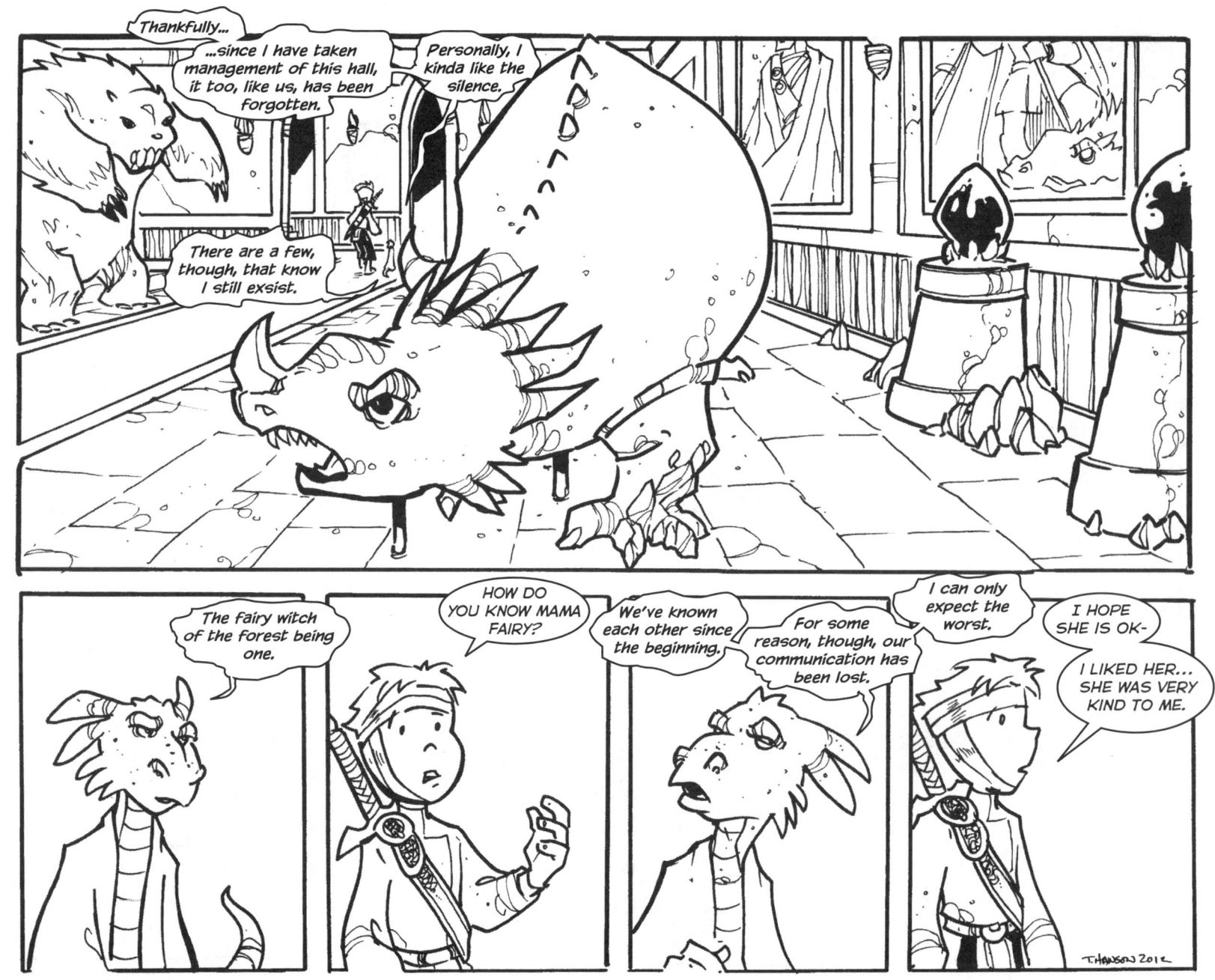

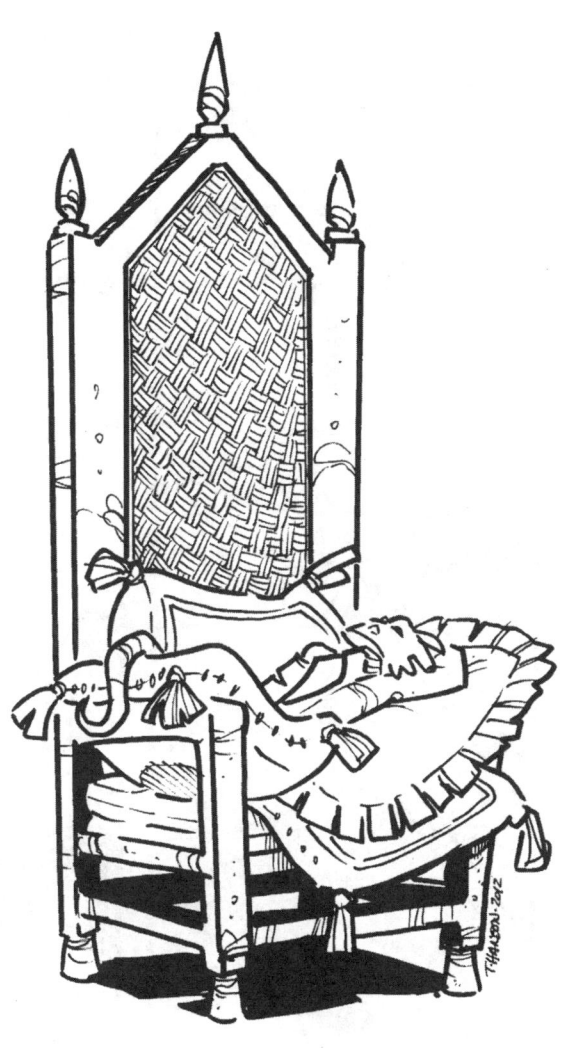

the Dragon Hunter

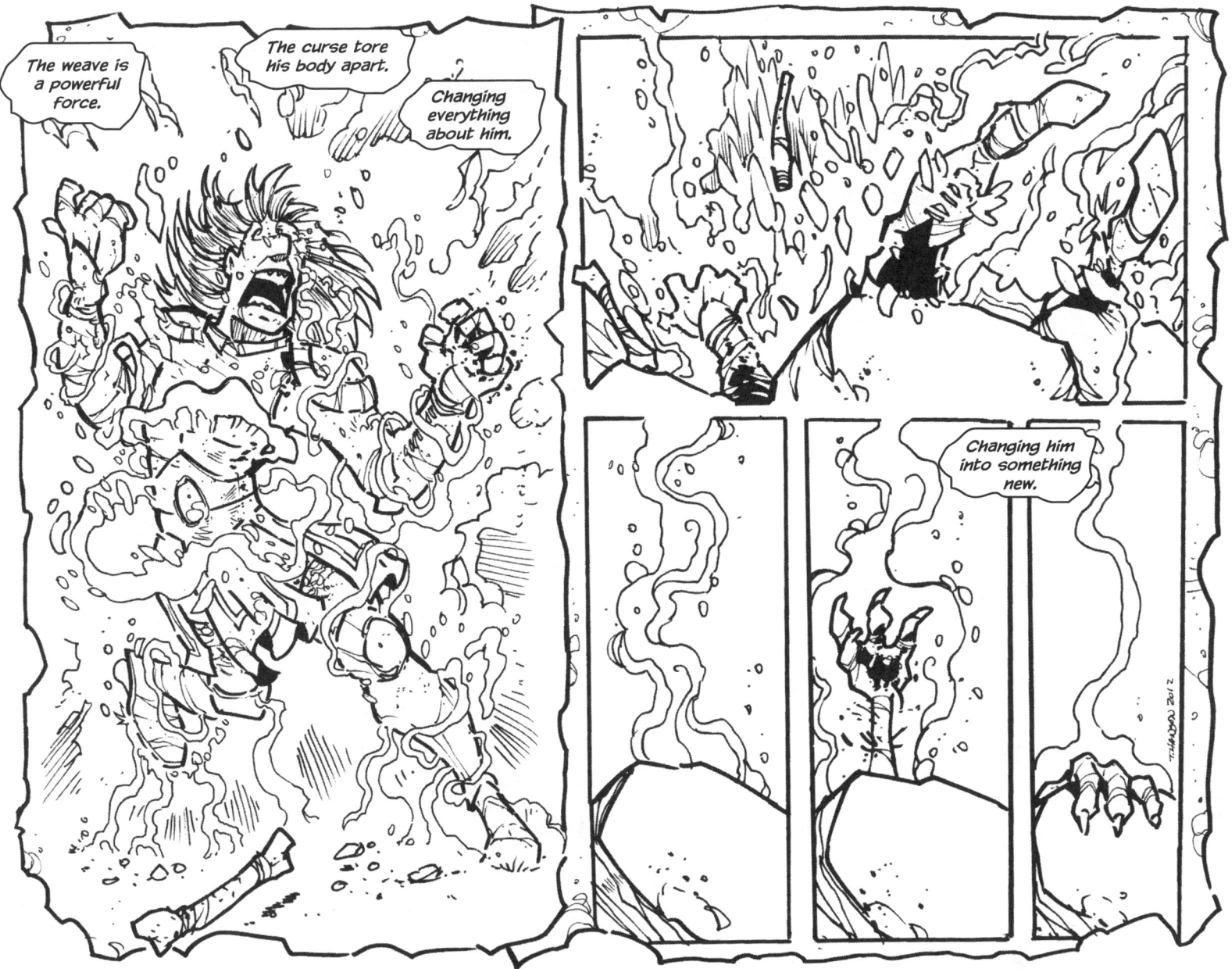

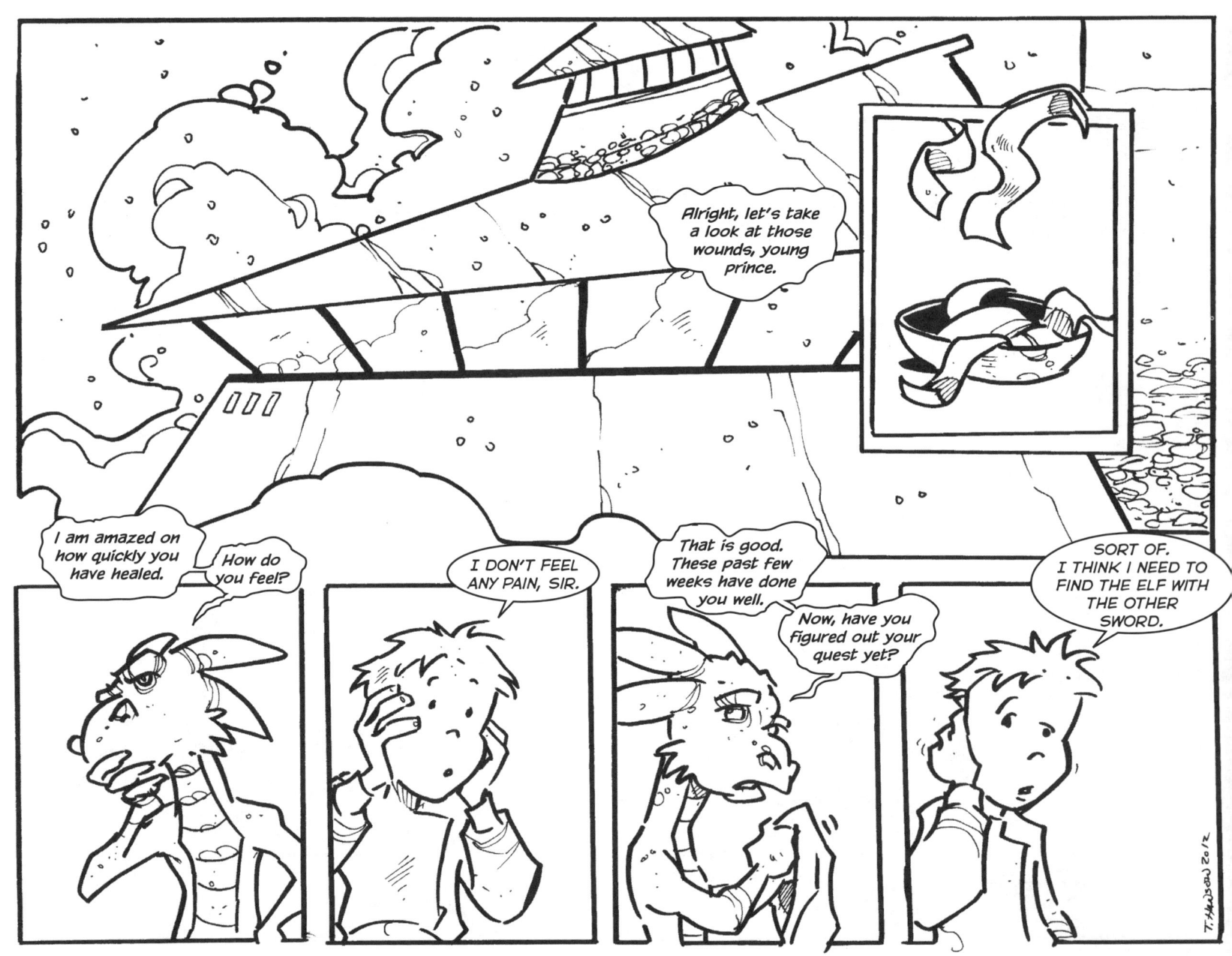

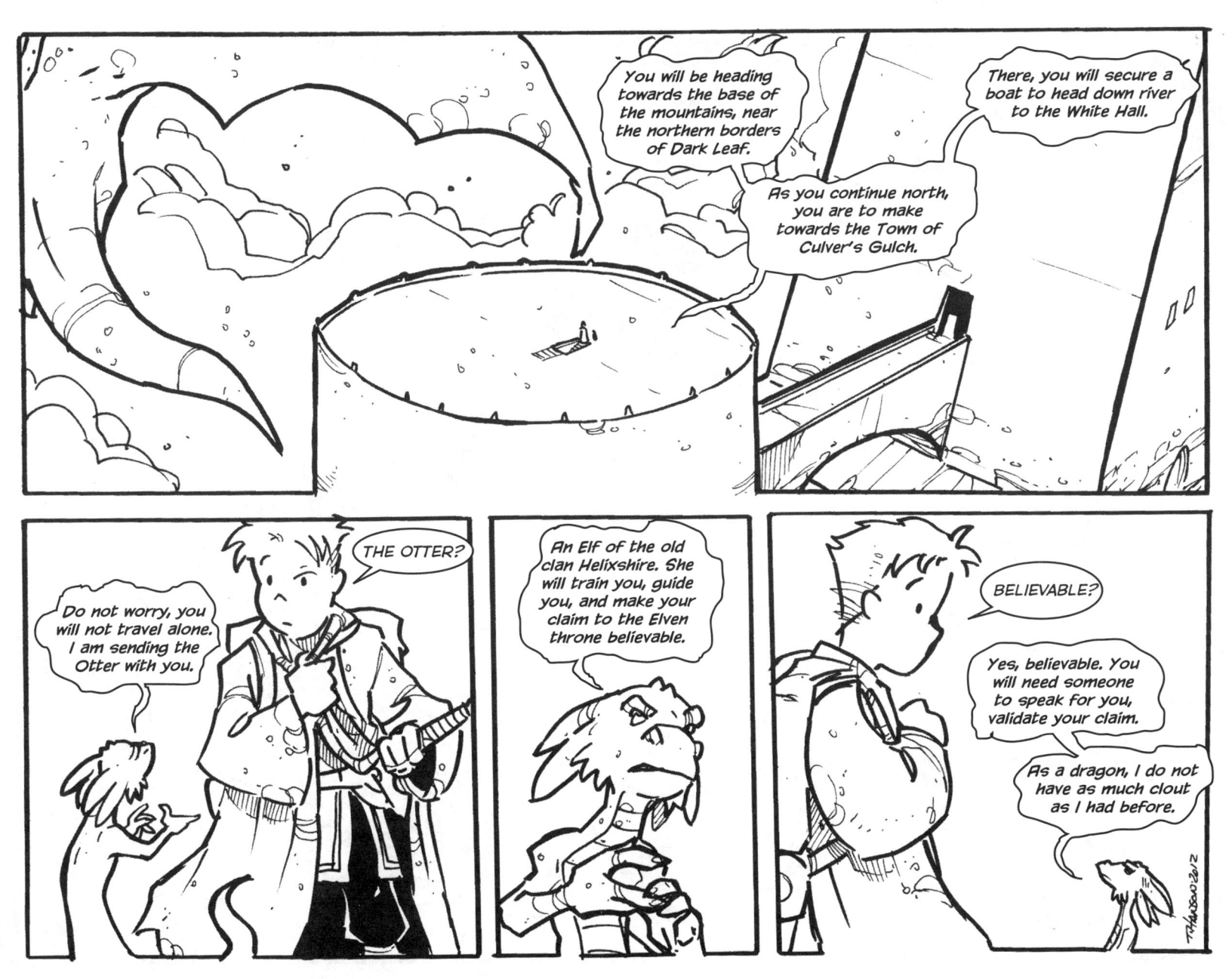

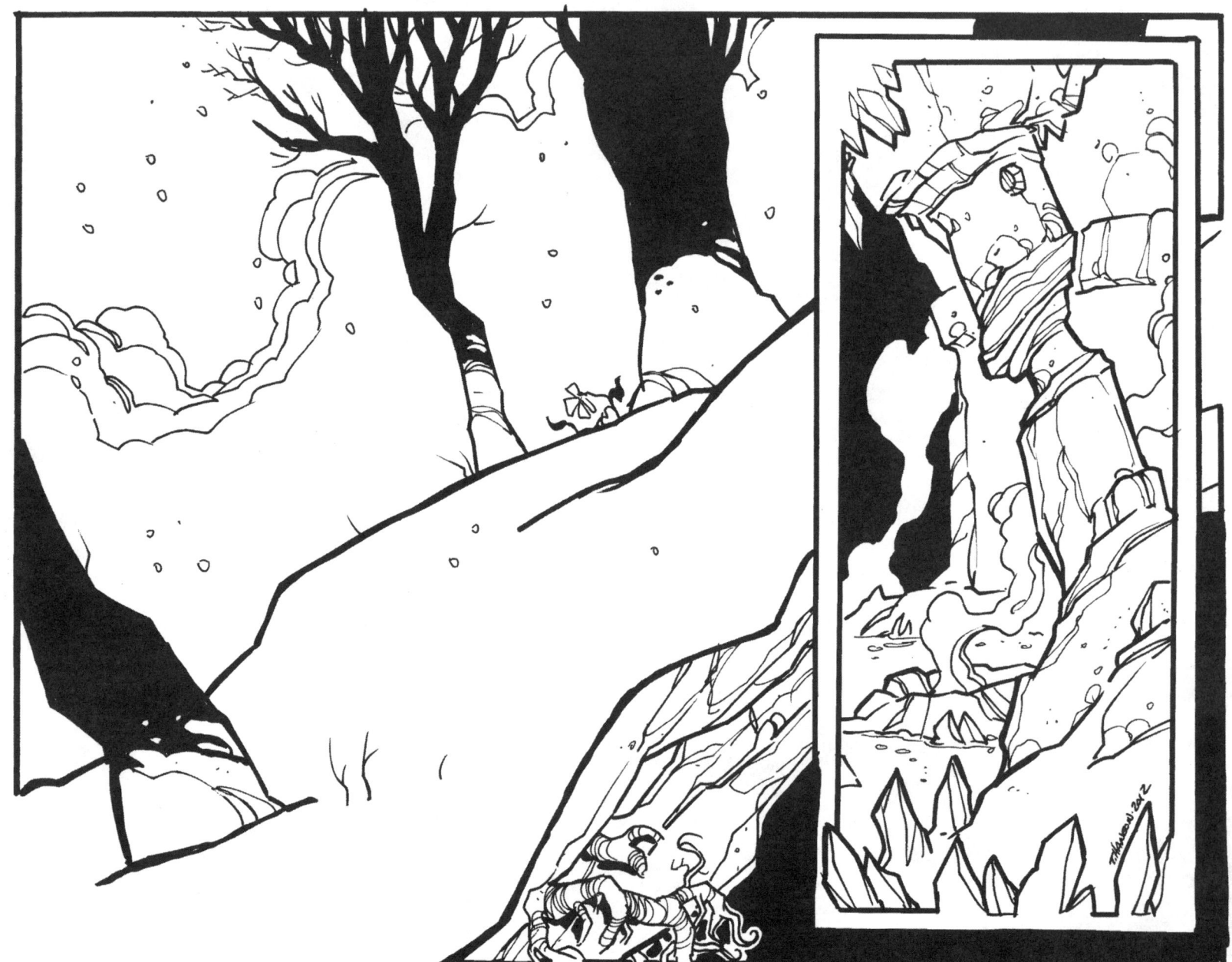

...must heal... must survive... must kill those that hurt me...

...all of them...

TO BE CONTINUED...

Thank you to the following people who made this dream possible. I could not have done this without your support.

Xephyr Inkpen
Dave Inkpen
Otmar, Dawn, Torin & Elyra
Schlunk
Sheila Lund
Brett "DJ Archangel" Strassner
D.J., Karen, Trae & Evan Cole
Bud, Jen, Ivy, Ian (Bean) Nebeker
Cavazos Flores
Gerolf Nikolay
Nathan and Melanie McConathy
DarkWaterSong

John Idlor
Brandon Eaker
Malin "Ravna" Runsten
Scantrontb
Timothy Drummond
Phill Layman
Sarah Morris
One Skunk Todd
David
Brandy Kuschel
Tenkokitsune
Ryan Busher

Tiggerperson
Terry Cook
Katherine and Elizabeth Rowe
Mike Collins
Anthony Dalo
B.A.D.
Punky Quiroz
Brenda Anderson
harvel
Geoff Bowers
Aylea & Jeff Allen
Furball
Christopher Daley
Bill Glasgow
Keith
Ed Ouano
Shane O'Dea
J. Patrick Walker
Julie Frost
Taylor Martin
John Bilderback
Tony Liang
Luke
Lee Cherolis
MAD
Joel M. Sones
Marc Angstadt
J Selsmark
Adrian Roberts
Dan Escobar
Drew & Leah

Jesper Nørskov Søndergaard
Michael Rawdon
Josh Flint
Kirpa Singh Gulati
Yin Yin
Pedro Velasco
Aaron "Dood" Edwards
Ivan Yagolnikov
Daryl Praeker
Sean McKay
James Quirk
Ed Kowalczewski
Chris Call
Ondrea Graye
Eric
Jason Lefler
Steve François Lefebvre
Kevin Ascott
Margaret St. John
Barnesy
T.S. DePree
Andrew Robbins
David Vazquez
finnsonc
Brian Sikkenga
SHL
David Workman
Karl Okerholm
Jdferries
Mathias Danielsson
Iain Mainprize
Howson

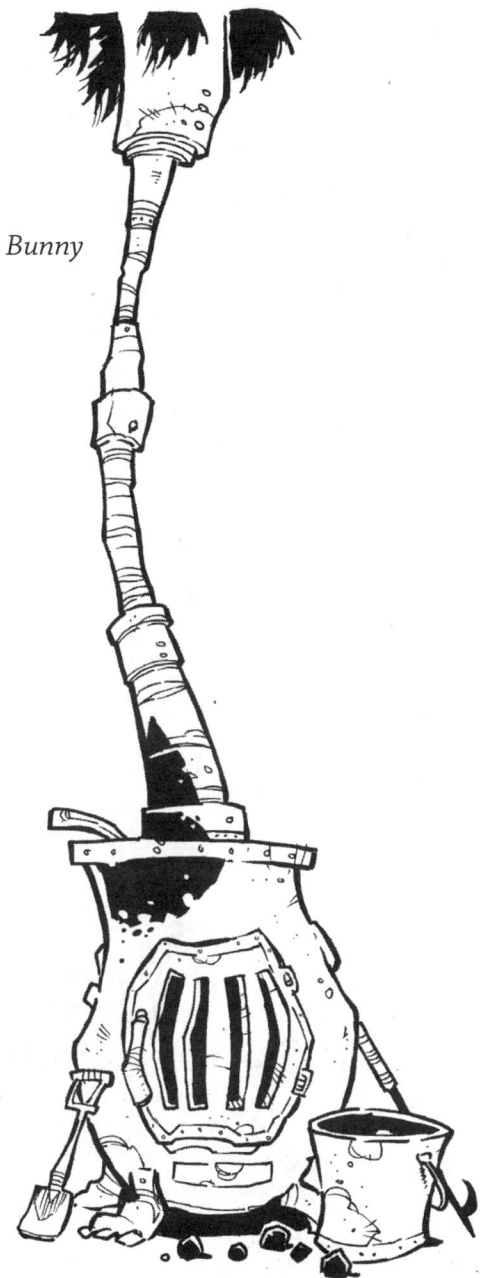

Jason Crossman	Rick Higginson	Georg Grosse-Hohl
Herman Choi	Edmund Widl	Calissa Moore
Verbamse	Syndi Keats	Dilraj Gill
Payne Family	Joel M. Waldron	Steve Hansen
Ross Demma	Mark DiBlasi	Ken Senter
Sarah Iozzio	Ken Malidore	Ben McCandless
Chip & Katie	Adam J. Monetta	Heidi Berthiaume & Bud the Bunny
Scott Murkin	Punmaster and Fantasmic	Lawrence Gill
Brett Abbott	Michael P. Chien	Brian Miller
Harald Demler	The Bain Family	Marc D. Long
David Bolick	Casey Bonanno	Christopher Ezold
Chris Young	C.Clemis	Gerald Campbell
Scott & Terry Hanson	Heather & Stephen Halliday	Zolgar
J.S."Jande"Rowe	Michael Whitmer	Amy Ratcliffe
Murray Wood	Wolfes	Sam Peacock
The Rich Family	Jordan Kotzebue	Cynthia Wood
Jeff Bolkovatz	James "Malveka" Allen	Windy Phipps
Dan " Dangur" Sudkamp	Lon Braidwood	Johnny Splendor
Michael Carson	Gregory A Sparks	Elonweis
The Hynes Family	Magnus Asplund	Susan Ator
The DUFFS from OZ	Kenneth Andersen - Kehaan	Frantz Family
CrisisSDK	Shahaan Dalal	Jeremy S
Alley Mann	Darren J Parker	Michael Jacob
Nolan & Holly Tolman & Family	Bill Brendle	Garvey Connelly
Felker Family	Greg Hatcher	Doug Sturtevant
Joshua Beale	Athena & Kyrie Goldman	Bibagana
Jason and Erin Schlueter	Eric Arsenault	Liam Simmons
Paul J. Smoogen	Amber Lanagan	Michael and Ruth Beaty
Mike Kunkel	Denise Gary	Tony Gullotti
The Butler Family	Sanne Muurling	Michael David Johas Teener
Rich Brown	Robert lilley	Kevin Pointer
Becci Van Hoosier	Kellie Rupard-Schorr	Raevyn Fletcher
	Niko Geyer	Jennifer Ryan

Chloe Sparkman
Steve Edwards
Jason Brubaker
Stephanie Williams-Mays
D. Huynh
Frank Sankot
Josh Maher
DamoWela
Trixie W
Stewart Kramp
Bryan
The Gang of Garcias
Jason Farrell
Niels Weiglin Knudsen
Robert Untucht
Richard McCalmont
Erin Paxton
Robin Dempsey
Rax
Steve Tracy
The Langs
Patrick C. Scullin

Jeremy Mai
Neil Bailey
Alberto Melendez
Curtis Bates
ReachTheSea.com
Tim Rogers
Don Koch
Mathieu Doublet
Jeff Zoet
Deborah Lang
JD Calderon
Gina
Kieran and Cameron Fisk
Thom Pratt
Austin Crawford
Kristin Lear
Jens Bejer Pedersen
Shari
Eric & Abby Hanson
Brian
Hannah S.
Jonathan Hepburn
Charlie Poulin
Cassandra Hanson Lloyd
Nate Lovett
Joshua H. Elias
Ali Enns
June Hanson
Daniel Bäumler
In Memory of Eileen Scott
Brian Juhl
Steve Lamperti
Arcane Snowman

~Saxony
Genevieve Gorta
Jonathon MacKenzie
Brett Grunig
Charles St. John Smith III
Purcell Family
Stephen Cook
Rich Clabaugh
Benjamin Strom
Damon English
Vince Bellows
Erin Hewett
C.M. Bean
The Frick Family
M. Rueckheim
Eddie Pittman
Jason Oren
William Weist
Roy Sutton
Peter Telchroeb
Val & Scott Brazier
Michael
Lee Keegan
Dennis W.
Anne Langston
Rachel Clark
Bindi Boyce
Dante
Eileen
Patrick Thunstrom
Darne Lang
Luke Keppler
Craig

Trenton Wynter Brown
Nicolas Fourcroy
Adam Baker-Siroty
Aaron Linde
The Rutters
Toby S.
R1artwork
Darrell Toland
Malia P
Nathan Rackley
Anabel Martinez
Jason King
Jouni Miettunen (Finland)
Michael Howard
Andy Owings
Roger Miró Salla
Emmy King
Hendrik Ebbers
Chris Tang
Aaron
Sreevidya Subramanian
Sara - Princess of the OOTG $7.77
The Mika Family
Mike Scigliano
Lustigit
Christoffer Rohrer
Ben Risbeck
Peter Cohen
Jared Saunders
Victor Briseno
John M. Trivilino
Lisa Jones
Dan F

Fergus Maximus
Gary Kacmarcik
Heather Marley
Silly McKinley's
Anders Lärka
Shawna Danea
JAMELAPO
Joshua Sloan
Noa & Tristan van Ladesteijn
Candra M.
Gijs
Silvernis
Noah Wexo
Anticia
Victoria D. Morris
Brian Stivers
Alice Bentley
Steve Espinas
Vonda Sargent
Ben Scarbeau
Mihnea Murgeanu
Edward Sizemore
Toon Verlinden
Howe Family
Fam. Fillafer
A. Baltazar
Amanda Ahlstrom
Martin Robaszewski
John Roberts
R. David Murray
Xavier Sala
J. Cebron Cook

Edmond Aggabao
Alex Khan
Eric Murphy
G
Mike Colston
Christopher C. Cockrell
David A. Watanabe
Chay D. Hart
Dougster
Lerolabell
Gabe McCann
Helena
Dave Baxter
Evan Gold
Christina
Peter Olson
Nick Poenn
Jim Kosmicki
Steven Lord
Reed
Kim Lapere
Keith Carnes
Kristopher Volter
Wouter F. Goedkoop
Scott Head
Domen Stojić

Garrett Fitzgerald
Joseph Hawkins
Katherine S.
Sarah Arrowsmith
Scratch9
Shawn Granger
Paul D.
Roy Cowing
Cheryl Naroski
Spencer Toyama
I Mainprize
Sara Patrick
Shirley
Baby Espinas

Travis Hanson-
Is an Eisner nominated illustrator with a huge imagination. Travis spends his time in Southern California, with his lovely wife Janell, Five children, two cats, one gecko, a bearded dragon and a bunch of fish in his reef tank.